**Please check all items for damages
before leaving the Library.
Thereafter you will be held
responsible for all injuries
to items beyond reasonable wear.**

Helen M. Plum Memorial Library

Lombard, Illinois

A daily fine will be charged for
overdue materials.

JUN   2015

ROMAN GLADIATORS

by Sheri Dillard

The Child's World®

Published by The Child's World®
1980 Lookout Drive • Mankato, MN 56003-1705
800-599-READ • www.childsworld.com

ACKNOWLEDGMENTS

The Child's World®: Mary Berendes, Publishing Director
Red Line Editorial: Editorial direction
The Design Lab: Design
Amnet: Production
Content Consultant: David Potter, Professor of Classics,
The University of Michigan
Design elements: iStockphoto
Photographs ©: Shutterstock Images, cover, 9; Veronika
Galkina/Shutterstock, 4, 30 (top right); Public Domain, 6;
Corbis, 10; Bettmann/Corbis, 12; Peter Hermes Furian/
Shutterstock Images, 13; Thinkstock, 17; Stapleton
Collection/Corbis, 18, 23, 30 (bottom right); Alinari Archives/
Corbis, 19, 30 (bottom left); Roger Wood/Corbis, 22; North
Wind Picture Archives, 27, 28; Vanni Archive/Corbis, 29

ISBN 9781631437588
LCCN 2014945426

Printed in the United States of America
Mankato, MN
November, 2014
PA02246

ABOUT THE AUTHOR

Sheri Dillard has written many stories for children. She has also worked as a preschool teacher. She lives in Atlanta, Georgia, with her husband, three sons, and a 100-pound puppy named Captain.

TABLE OF CONTENTS

The Roman Colosseum still stands in Rome, Italy.

CHAPTER ONE

THE OPENING GAMES

In 80 AD, the Roman Colosseum was completed. It had taken nearly ten years to build. This was the largest **amphitheater** ever built in the empire. The **emperor** wanted to celebrate. He ordered a grand event with 100 days of gladiator games. More than 50,000 people attended. The main event on opening day was a fight between two of Rome's best gladiators: Verus and Priscus.

As Verus walked toward the arena, he heard sounds all around him. He heard the scraping of weapons being sharpened. He heard the growls of wild animals as they paced in their cages. Trumpets blared. The crowd roared.

Verus also heard the groans of injured gladiators. He walked past stretchers lined up for the wounded. Gladiator

A Roman mosaic shows a variety of gladiators in combat.

battles were not ordinary sporting events. They were brutal fights that often ended in death.

Verus and Priscus were both skilled fighters. The fight lasted a very long time. This battle was the only gladiator fight recorded in detail. The Roman poet Martial described the brave and heroic battle. It was such a good fight that the spectators cheered for both men to win. But Emperor Titus followed the rules of a gladiator battle. The fight continued until one of the men gave up. Verus and Priscus **conceded** their defeat at the same time. And the emperor declared them both winners. Verus and Priscus each received a wooden sword. This sword meant they could leave the arena as free men.

Forced to Fight

There were many slaves in ancient Rome. Some slaves worked in rock quarries, farms, or homes. Some slaves were gladiators. They were forced to fight. A slave owner made money by renting his gladiators for battles at games. It was a risky business, though. A gladiator might become badly wounded and die during a game.

Another View
A chance to be free

A *rudis* was a wooden sword. When a gladiator was awarded a *rudis*, he became a free man. Some gladiators were given one for having many victories. Others earned their freedom during an exciting victory. Retired gladiators could become trainers for other gladiators. Or they became bodyguards for the wealthy. But some continued to battle as free men. This type of gladiator was called a *rudiarius*. Why do you think retired gladiators wanted to return to fighting?

CHAPTER TWO

GLADIATOR HISTORY

The time of the Roman gladiator spanned almost
700 years. The first recorded fight was in 264 BC.
The last known battle was in the early fifth century AD.
Ancient Rome was brutal and violent. Gladiator battles
were similar to mock wars. The gladiator fights were
symbols of the Roman values of bravery and honor.

Gladiator fights came from an Etruscan funeral
ritual. Etruscans were a powerful people in Italy who
lived there before the Romans. When an army leader
died, his warriors honored him. They fought near his
grave. The spilled blood was an offering to his spirit.

This ritual was later changed. When a wealthy
person died, slaves or war prisoners fought at the

For centuries, the Roman Forum was the center of public life in Rome.

funeral. The first gladiator fight in Rome was at the funeral of a wealthy **aristocrat**. The fight was held at a public cattle market. It drew a large crowd. Fights soon became political events. Aristocrats held them to show their power.

Gladiator fights quickly became popular. Fights were held in public spaces, such as the Roman Forum. This forum was the center of activity in ancient Rome. There were shops, markets, government buildings, and

A gladiator wins his battles against several other gladiators.

religious buildings. The gladiator battles were held in a large open area. There were wooden stands for seating.

There was a need for a large, permanent place for gladiator battles. An amphitheater was designed for gladiator events. An amphitheater was oval shaped. The arena was in the center. This was where the fighting took place. Seating was around the arena. The first amphitheater was built in Pompeii, Italy, in the first century BC. Around 70 AD, construction started on the amphitheater in Rome. This amphitheater is now called the Colosseum. It was built just over 1 mile (1.6 km) east of the Roman Forum. The Colosseum could hold more than 50,000 people. Over time, more than 250 amphitheaters were built throughout the Roman Empire.

Emperors held **elaborate** gladiator games. Some lasted more than 100 days. These events were very popular. People packed together tightly in the seats. The games were free to attend. This entertainment was a gift paid for by the emperor. The emperor attended the games, too. It was a rare time when the emperor was with the Roman people. He gained his followers'

The emperor and audience watched as
gladiators fought in an arena.

At its height in 117 AD, the Roman Empire stretched
across Europe to parts of the Middle East and Africa.
This map shows ancient Roman place names.

support. The people saw the emperor's power and the strength of the empire.

Soon Christianity spread throughout the empire. Then the gladiator games became less popular. The games went against Christian teachings. Many Christians thought the games were cruel. Constantine I ruled from 312 to 337 AD. He was the first Roman emperor to become a Christian.

Emperor Honorius ruled from 393 to 423 AD. During that time, a Christian monk ran into the arena during a gladiator event. He pleaded for gladiator battles to end. The crowd grew angry and the monk was killed. But his efforts made the emperor wonder if the games were good for the people. Soon after, Emperor Honorius announced the end of the gladiator games. Gladiator games ended in the early fifth century.

The Colosseum

The Colosseum took approximately ten years to build. It was completed in 80 AD. It covered 6 acres (2.4 hectares) and had 80 entrances. Not only gladiator battles were held there. Colosseum events also included **chariot** races and wild animal hunts. Sometimes staged naval battles took place in the arena. It was filled with water. Today, the Roman Colosseum is a popular tourist spot. Millions of people visit each year.

Another View
VOLUNTEER GLADIATORS

Some gladiators were volunteers. They chose to become gladiators because they needed money to pay debts. Other volunteers wanted the chance to be famous and successful. But the sport was very dangerous. Some gladiators died in battle. Others were badly wounded. How would you feel if a family member chose to be a gladiator?

CHAPTER THREE

WEAPONS AND ARMOR

Most gladiators wore simple **loincloths** or tunics.
Gladiators usually wore nothing on their chests. They
wore sandals or went barefoot. But not all gladiators
looked the same. There were many types of gladiators.
They each had unique weapons and armor. Some were
prisoners of war. They were named after the region they
came from. Some were named after their fighting style.
Different types of gladiators were matched up to make
a fight more interesting. The *murmillo*, *retiarius*, and
Thracian gladiators were three of the most popular types.

The *murmillo*, a fish fighter, was a well-protected
gladiator. His large helmet had a fish crest and a fin.

A long shield provided good protection, but it was heavy and difficult to manage. A *murmillo* gladiator also wore metal armor. This **greave** was worn on his leg. Most gladiators were right-handed. They held their shields with their left hands. The greave helped protect body parts that the shield did not

A *murmillo* gladiator fought with a short sword.

cover. A *murmillo* fought with a sword.

A *retiarius*, a net fighter, was equipped with items that a fisherman might use. He had a net, a trident, and a dagger. A *retiarius* did not have much armor. But this allowed him to move around quickly and easily. He wore no helmet. His only armor was a metal plate on his left shoulder.

A *retiarius* gladiator used his net and trident
to attack other gladiators.

A beast hunter fought animals, such as leopards.

The Thracian gladiator was named after Thrace.
This was an area in Europe that now includes parts
of Bulgaria, Greece, and Turkey. Thracians were early
enemies of Rome. Some Thracian gladiators were
prisoners of war. Thracian gladiators wore helmets and
fought with curved swords. They used small, round
shields and wore greaves on their legs.

Spartacus

Spartacus was a gladiator from Thrace. He led a slave **rebellion** in 73 BC. More than 70 other gladiators joined Spartacus. The gladiators had been trained to fight and were physically fit. They fought against the Roman army. Spartacus and his men easily defeated the first group of Roman soldiers to attack them. The slave rebellion grew to include more than 100,000 men. They had many victories during the first year, but the Roman army was too powerful. Spartacus and his men were ultimately defeated in 71 BC.

Another View
The Gladiator Business

Many people made money from the gladiator business. Wealthy Romans owned or invested in a group of gladiators. Betting on gladiator fights was common. Gladiator owners made money by renting out their men. And staging gladiator events was a way for politicians to earn followers. Staging a gladiator event could bring power and wealth. What do you think gladiators thought about other people making money from their battles?

CHAPTER FOUR

BATTLE TACTICS

Sometimes a gladiator battle included just two gladiators in the arena. Other events put many gladiators in the arena at once. These group battles used newer gladiators. They opened for a main event. Or a group of gladiators acted out a victory of the Roman army.

Each gladiator type had a different battle style with strengths and weaknesses. A heavily armored gladiator was well protected, but he might move slowly because of his armor's weight. A lightly armored **opponent** could move around quickly and easily, but parts of his body were more vulnerable to attack.

A *retiarius* gladiator used his net to trap or trip his opponent. A *retiarius* was not weighed down by heavy

Battle styles varied by gladiator types.

armor. He moved around quickly and easily. He used his long trident to injure opponents from a distance. But he used his dagger when a gladiator was trapped or tangled in his net.

A *murmillo* was very well protected. His helmet covered his entire head and face with only small slits to see through. His rectangular shield protected him, and its heavy weight could also injure his opponent. He used his sword to thrust and jab.

The Thracian was lightly armored, so he could move around with great speed. He fought with a short, curved sword called a *sica*. He used the *sica* as a slashing weapon. To defend himself, he used a small shield.

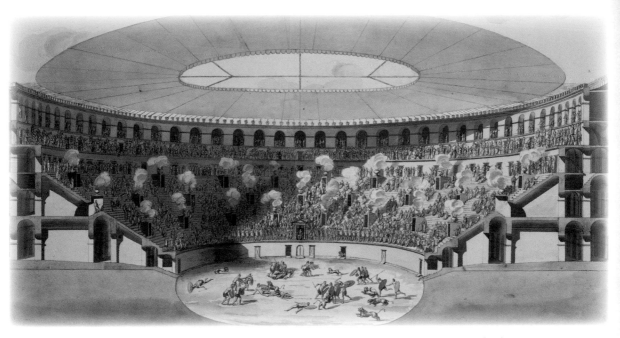

Different wild beast hunts happened at the same time at an amphitheater.

Left-handed gladiators had an advantage. Most gladiators were right-handed. Because of this, most gladiators trained to fight against right-handed fighters. But left-handed fighters attacked from a different angle. Many gladiators were not prepared to fight against a left-handed fighter. This made fights with left-handed fighters hard to predict.

A few types of gladiators had especially unusual fighting methods. *Andabatae* wore helmets that covered their eyes completely. They fought blind. *Dimacheri* had no shield and fought with a sword in each hand. *Laquerarii* used ropes to catch their opponents.

Gladiator battles had many rules. A referee made sure that the rules were followed. A wounded gladiator could ask for mercy by raising a finger to his opponent or the referee. Sometimes the crowd's reaction influenced a gladiator's fate. If the crowd turned their thumbs, the audience wanted a gladiator to be killed. The emperor made the final decision. If he thought the gladiator fought well, the gladiator's life might be spared. If a gladiator won many battles over his career, the emperor might award him a *rudis* to make the gladiator a free man. Many retired gladiators became trainers at gladiator schools.

Gladiator Schools

Gladiators lived and trained in gladiator schools called *ludus*. The men ate, trained, and slept in dorm-like prisons as they prepared to fight as gladiators. They had long training sessions, often with retired gladiators. They practiced battling with wooden swords. The training was rough, but the gladiators were fed well and had excellent medical care.

Another View
Unusual Fighters

Venatores, the hunters, were beast fighters. The *venatores* entered the ring on horseback. Another type of gladiator was the *essedarii*, who rode into arenas on chariots. The *essedarii* sometimes fought from their chariots and sometimes fought on foot. How might a gladiator feel about fighting only according to his type and battle tools?

CHAPTER FIVE

GAMES AT THE COLOSSEUM

The festivals held in the Colosseum were grand events. They celebrated important events and the power of the Roman Empire.

The opening day of gladiator games usually started with a parade through the streets of Rome. Slaves dressed in costumes. Musicians, chariots, acrobats, dancers, and trainers with their wild animals made their way toward the Colosseum. Once inside, the gladiators joined them. They all circled around the arena. Then the gladiators presented themselves to the emperor.

The first events were staged animal hunts and fights. Lions, tigers, elephants, hippopotamuses, bears, and many other types of animals were brought in from all over the Roman Empire. These events were exciting

The opening event of gladiator games included animals.

for the people to watch. Many had never seen the exotic animals before. The animals were sent into the arena, and the *venatores* hunted them with spears and bows and arrows. Thousands of animals died in the opening games at the Colosseum. Animal fights were sometimes used as a way to execute criminals. Unlike the *venatores*, the criminals did not have weapons or any way to defend themselves, so the animals usually killed them.

The gladiator battles came last and were the highlight of each day of a festival. During the many

Some gladiators rode in on chariots and horses.

days of a festival, thousands of gladiators fought. The emperor decided who died and who was spared. The victor was celebrated. He became well known in Rome and throughout the empire. The battles were also a time for the emperor to be among his people. His event entertained them. He showed his wealth. Many times, the audience stood and clapped for their emperor.

Although gladiator battles entertained Roman people, they were full of violence and death. Like a soldier, a gladiator needed to be brave. For the people of ancient Rome, gladiator fights displayed treasured Roman values.

Not Everyone Was a Fan

Not everyone enjoyed gladiator battles. Emperor Marcus Aurelius found them boring. Some philosophers spoke out against the practice. They criticized how poorly the Roman people behaved during battles. The mob shouted to kill the gladiators. Spectators could influence a leader's decision about whether a gladiator was killed or spared after a fight. The Roman philosopher Seneca was also against the events. He worried about people spending their free time at the violent events.

Marcus Aurelius ruled the Roman Empire from 161 to 180 AD.

Another View
Violent Entertainment

In ancient Rome, families went to the gladiator games for entertainment. The games were free, and men, women, and children could all attend. Violence was common in ancient Rome, and this sort of entertainment was not seen as unusual. Young children saw humans and animals injured and sometimes killed. What effect do you think this might have had on children?

TIMELINE

264
BC

The first recorded gladiator fight occurs in Rome.

73
BC

Spartacus leads a slave rebellion with more than 70 gladiators.

71
BC

Spartacus and his army are defeated.

70
AD

The Roman Colosseum construction begins.

80

The Roman Colosseum opens with 100 days of games.

312

Emperor Constantine I becomes Rome's first Christian emperor and rules until 337.

Early Fifth century

Gladiator games end.

GLOSSARY

amphitheater (AM-fi-thee-uh-ter) An amphitheater is a large, open building with rows of seats around an arena in the middle. The Roman Colosseum was the empire's largest amphitheater.

aristocrat (uh-RISS-tuh-krat) An aristocrat is someone who belongs to a group of people in society who have more money and power than others. An aristocrat might sponsor a gladiator battle to gain followers.

chariot (CHA-ree-uht) A chariot is a small vehicle that is pulled by one or more horses and was often used in battle in ancient times. Some gladiator events included chariot races.

conceded (kuhn-SEED-id) To have conceded is to have admitted that you did not win a battle. Both Verus and Priscus conceded their defeat at the same time.

elaborate (i-LAB-ur-it) Something that is elaborate is complicated and detailed. Gladiator games were elaborate events.

emperor (EM-pur-or) An emperor is the male ruler of a society. Gladiator games were paid for by the emperor.

greave (GREEV) A greave is armor worn on the leg between the knee and the ankle. Certain gladiators wore a greave into battle.

loincloths (LOYN-kloths) Loincloths are pieces of cloth worn over the lower torso to cover private areas of the body. Many gladiators wore loincloths.

opponent (uh-POH-nuhnt) An opponent is someone who fights against another in a sport or battle. A *retiarius* gladiator used his net to trap or trip his opponent.

rebellion (ri-BEL-yuhn) A rebellion is a struggle against a government or other group in charge. Spartacus led a rebellion with other gladiators against the Roman army.

ritual (RICH-oo-uhl) A ritual is a set of actions that are always performed in the same way as part of a religious ceremony. Gladiator battles started out as a part of a funeral ritual.

TO LEARN MORE

BOOKS

James, Simon. *Eyewitness Ancient Rome.*
New York: DK Publishing, 2008.

Lacey, Minna, and Susanna Davidson. *Gladiators.*
London, UK: Usborne, 2006.

Park, Louise, and Timothy Love. *The Roman Gladiators.*
New York: Marshall Cavendish Benchmark, 2010.

WEB SITES

Visit our Web site for links about Roman gladiators:

childsworld.com/links

Note to Parents, Teachers, and Librarians: We routinely verify our Web links to make sure they are safe and active sites. So encourage your readers to check them out!

INDEX